SNOWBOARD DUEL

BY JAKE MADDOX

illustrated by Sean Tiffany

text by Bob Temple

Librarian Reviewer
Chris Kreie
Media Specialist, Eden Prairie Schools, MN
MS in Information Media, St. Cloud State University, MN

Reading Consultant
Mary Evenson
Middle School Teacher, Edina Public Schools, MN
MA in Education, University of Minnesota

STONE ARCH BOOKS
Minneapolis San Diego

Jake Maddox Books are published by Stone Arch Books,
A Capstone Imprint
1710 Roe Crest Drive
North Mankato, Minnesota 56003
www.capstonepub.com

Library of Congress Cataloging-in-Publication Data
Maddox, Jake.
    Snowboard Duel / by Jake Maddox; illustrated by Sean Tiffany.
    p. cm. — (Impact Books. A Jake Maddox Sports Story)
    Summary: When the son of the new manager of the ski resort
starts a snowboard cross team and will not allow girls to join, Brian and
Hannah try to think of a way to change his mind.
    ISBN-13: 978-1-59889-843-9 (library binding)
    ISBN-10: 1-59889-843-4 (library binding)
    ISBN-13: 978-1-59889-895-8 (paperback)
    ISBN-10: 1-59889-895-7 (paperback)
    [1. Snowboarding—Fiction. 2. Competition (Psychology)—Fiction.
3. Discrimination—Fiction.] I. Tiffany, Sean, ill. II. Title.
PZ7.M25643Sn 2008
[Fic]—dc22   2007003634

Art Director: Heather Kindseth
Graphic Designer: Kay Fraser

Printed in the United States of America in Stevens Point, Wisconsin.
082013
007679R

TABLE OF CONTENTS

NEW RULES

The door of the school bus had barely closed behind him, and Brian was on his way to the chalet.

It was the way Brian ended almost every school day, jumping off the bus and heading at full speed to the slopes.

Brian's mother was the assistant manager of Snowstream Ski Resort. That meant Brian had easy access to the resort's many cool features.

Each day, he would head directly to the chalet. He would open his locker and pull out his snowboard gear. He would rush to put it on, and would get to the slopes as quickly as he could.

On the slopes, he would meet his friends. Almost all of them were kids whose parents worked at the resort. Most of them were about Brian's age, and they all were snowboarders.

Some days were spent at the halfpipe, working on a front side 720 or another special trick. Other days were spent grinding the rails down the slopes.

No matter what they were doing, Brian and his friends were happy.

Brian often snowboarded until dark. Then he would head home for a late dinner and homework before bed.

The next morning, the whole thing would start over.

It was a great life.

Brian swung by his mother's office to say hello before he headed for the chairlift. He bolted toward the office on the top floor of the chalet.

"Hey, Mom," Brian said as he came through the door.

"Hi, Brian," his mom responded. She seemed a little busy.

"I'm going to the halfpipe today, okay?" Brian said.

"Okay," she said, barely looking up from her papers. "Have fun."

His mom had been busy a lot since the resort manager retired three months ago.

They hadn't replaced him yet, and it meant that Brian's mom had a lot of extra work to do.

Brian grabbed his board on the deck of the chalet and bounced down the steps toward the snow. He stepped into his board and latched the right boot in place. Pushing along the snow with his left foot, he glided down toward the chairlift.

His best friend, Hannah, was there waiting for him. "Hey, Bri," she said. Hannah seemed a little distracted.

The lifts weren't busy, so Brian and Hannah got on a chair quickly. Once they were up in the air, Brian started asking questions.

"You okay?" he said. "You seem a little down."

"Well, didn't you hear the news? Didn't your mom tell you?" Hannah asked.

"Tell me what?" Brian asked.

"I ran into my dad on my way here," Hannah said. Hannah's father ran the restaurant in the chalet. "I guess the resort hired a new manager," Hannah added.

"Oh, good!" Brian said. "My mom's been waiting for that. Maybe now she won't have to work so much."

"I don't know about that," Hannah said. "My dad said the new manager's not a very nice person. She's making a bunch of new rules right away."

"Like what?" Brian said.

"Like, we may not be able to snowboard for free anymore," she said.

THE BOY IN THE BLUE HELMET

Brian sat quietly on the chair for a few moments.

It was a crisp, calm day. The growing chill he was feeling was not from the weather.

"What do you mean?" he finally asked.

Hannah glanced across the slopes. Below them, skiers were swooshing down the mountain through the soft, fluffy snow that had fallen only hours earlier.

"Being able to use the resort for free is a benefit that our parents have, and we have, because of their jobs," Hannah said.

"I know that, but why would they take it away?" Brian said.

"I don't know," Hannah said. "All I know is what my dad told me. The new manager said she wanted to make some changes to the benefits that the families of the employees get."

Silence again fell over the chairlift. Hannah and Brian could see the end of the chairlift now.

They both wondered if they were soon going to see the end of their time on the slopes, too.

Then Brian said what both of them were thinking.

"But if we lose the free snowboarding," he said, "what are we going to do all winter? What else are we going to do up here on this mountain?"

Hannah just shook her head.

Both of them slipped off the chairlift and pushed over to the top of the nearby halfpipe.

At the edge of the pipe, they paused and looked at each other.

They both shook their heads and started down the run.

As soon as they swooped down one side of the halfpipe, their minds were free again.

Brian led the way as they played a game they called Chase.

They had played many times before.

One of them would go out front and do a trick on each side of the pipe.

The other would follow behind, watching and trying to match everything the leader did.

Chase was a game they had been playing for two winters, ever since both of their parents had been hired at Snowstream.

Hannah and Brian loved the game so much that they didn't even have to talk about playing it anymore.

If they were at the halfpipe, they were playing Chase.

On the first run, Brian didn't try anything too hard, but their first time down was usually pretty tame.

Hannah didn't have much trouble matching Brian, trick for trick. She rarely did anyway.

Hannah was as good a snowboarder as Brian was.

There were a few tricks he could do better and a few she could do better.

When they got to the bottom of the run, they came together and gave each other a high five.

"Sweet run," Hannah said. "Next time, I lead."

They looked up the halfpipe and talked about the tricks they had tried and how they had done.

Suddenly, however, there was a new figure at the top of the halfpipe.

It was hard to see who it was from the bottom of the run, but the person didn't look familiar to Hannah and Brian.

He wore a full, dark-blue snowboarding suit, with a helmet to match.

Hannah and Brian watched the new boy's run.

He zoomed back and forth on the halfpipe at top speed.

At each turn, he performed a different trick, making each one look more effortless than the one before it.

It was a beautiful run.

At the bottom of the run, the boy zoomed up to Hannah and Brian.

He leaned back on his board to come to a stop.

Snow flew all over their boots in the process.

"Nice run!" Hannah said politely.

"Hmph," the boy snorted back. "That's not much of a halfpipe."

MAKING CHANGES

Brian and Hannah glanced at each other, shocked.

They weren't sure they heard the boy right, and they weren't sure what to say to him.

"I'm sorry, is there something wrong?" Brian said, still trying to be polite.

"Yeah, I'd say so," the boy said. "Your halfpipe is weak."

Hannah looked the boy up and down.

He was tall, and looked a little older than them.

His snowboarding suit was perfectly matched and looked nearly brand new and expensive.

The pants and the jacket both had the same logo: Blair Mountain Ski Resort.

This wasn't regular clothing you could buy at the resort, either. It looked like some kind of team outfit.

Both Hannah and Brian recognized it.

Blair Mountain was one of the best and most expensive resorts in the Rocky Mountains.

Neither Hannah nor Brian had ever been there.

But they both had talked about how cool it would be to go and snowboard there someday.

The ski runs were supposed to be twice as long as the ones at Snowstream.

The boy's board was top of the line, too. Hannah and Brian didn't have the gear that this new boy had.

They both wore red Snowstream jackets, but they were the normal kind you could find at a store. Nothing special.

Their snowboard pants didn't match their coats, and they had been bought from a discount store on the Internet.

Their boards were average brands, too.

None of that had ever mattered to Brian and Hannah until this boy showed up.

Both of them felt a little jealous of the boy, but they weren't ready to accept the insult to their home.

"Weak?" Hannah said. "It may not be Blair Mountain, but we like it here."

"Well, we need to make some changes," the boy said.

Now Brian was getting angry. "We? We need to make some changes?"

"That's what I said," the boy said. "We need to make some changes around here."

The boy reached down and unstrapped his snowboard from his back leg.

He began to push down toward the chairlift again.

Brian and Hannah looked at each other in amazement.

Neither one of them was sure what to do next.

Brian headed after the boy. "Excuse me," he yelled.

The boy kept walking to the chairlift.

"Excuse me!" Brian shouted.

This time, the boy stopped.

"Just who the heck do you think you are, hotshot?" Brian asked. He could feel that his face was red with anger.

The boy spun back with a sly smile on his face.

"I'm Zach," he said. "My mom is the new manager here. And like I said, we need to make a few changes."

CHAPTER 4

FREE NO MORE

Suddenly, Brian and Hannah didn't feel much like boarding.

They glided back to the chalet and unstrapped their snowboards. Then they stomped up the back steps to the chalet's deck, took off their boots, and went inside.

They spent the rest of the afternoon sitting by the fire in the chalet, talking about this new boy and what the new rules might mean.

"We need some kind of a plan," Brian said.

"How can we make a plan if we don't know what's going to happen yet?" Hannah said. "We should be patient and see what he's up to, then make our plan." Brian agreed.

Gradually, all of their other friends started to show up in the chalet. Ray, B.J., and Will had each already had some kind of run-in with Zach. They were all looking for information about what might be happening. And they wanted to share their stories with friends.

"He asked me if I could grind the rails on the snowboard runs," Ray said. "I said yes and then showed him. When I got to the bottom of the hill, he was laughing at me."

The others had similar stories.

No one was sure what to make of it. But they all figured they'd find out soon enough.

* * *

That night at home, Brian tried to talk to his mom about Zach.

She was sympathetic, but said there wasn't much that could be done just yet.

"I'm sure he's just trying to look cool in his new home," she said. "He'll tone it down once he gets to know all of you."

Brian wasn't so sure.

"He keeps talking about changes," Brian said. "And Hannah told me that her dad said we might lose our right to free snowboarding. Is that true?"

"I don't know yet, Brian," his mom said. She sighed. "But I'm sure that some things will change. Things always change when there is a new manager. It's nothing to worry about."

But Brian was still worried.

* * *

After school the next day, he and Hannah met at the resort again.

They walked into the locker room and got ready to snowboard.

On their way out to the slopes, however, they saw Zach inside the chalet.

He was putting up a sign on the bulletin board. In bold letters, it read:

TEEN SNOWBOARD CROSS

TEAM SIGN-UP

There was an empty space below it for people to put their names.

Hannah and Brian were confused, because Snowstream didn't have a snowboard cross course on it.

But they were both excited, too. They had always wanted to try snowboard cross. The idea of racing against other people down a twisting, turning snowboard run sounded pretty cool.

Hannah saw it as a chance to be nice to Zach. "Hey, Zach. So you're starting a snowboard cross team? Here at Snowstream?" she asked him.

"Yeah," he said. He didn't seem interested in her questions. "I was captain of the team at Blair Mountain. We were winners. Even though I'm stuck at this resort now, I still want to win."

Hannah and Brian tried to ignore the nasty part of Zach's comments.

"Sounds like fun," Brian said.

"It's awesome," Zach said. "My mom said we're going to take one of the ski runs and turn it into a snowboard cross course. We'll be able to start practicing in a few weeks. And I'm the captain."

GETTING AIR

Hannah and Brian started to feel a little differently about Zach after they found out about the snowboard cross team.

They weren't sure they liked the idea of Zach being the captain. But they thought being on the team would be fun.

They were the first two people to put their names on the sign-up sheet.

Ray, B.J., and Will all signed up, too.

For the next couple of weeks, the mood at Snowstream was better.

Every day after school, and all day on weekends, the kids snowboarded on the slopes and the halfpipe.

Their worries about changes to the rules about free skiing were gone.

After all, if Snowstream was starting a teen snowboard cross team, they would have to allow those kids to use the resort.

Brian and Hannah didn't see much of Zach.

When they did, he was over on the run that was being turned into a snowboard cross course.

The area had been closed to the public. It looked like Zach was helping the workers test the course.

Finally, one day they arrived at the slopes to find the snowboard cross course open. They couldn't wait to give it a try.

They rushed to get their snowboard suits and boots on, and quickly headed toward the chairlifts.

"Have you heard anything about it?" Hannah asked as they rode up the side of the mountain.

"Not much," Brian said. "My mom said it was going to be really hard. That's all I know."

"Sounds fun to me!" Hannah said.

Brian couldn't remember a time when he saw her so excited.

When they got to the drop-off point for the chairlift, Hannah cruised over toward the top of the course.

Brian struggled to keep up. "Wait up!" he yelled.

"Not a chance," Hannah shot back. "I'm not letting you take the course first!"

"Well," Brian responded, "it is a race course. Maybe you and I should have a little race!"

Hannah wasn't going to miss a chance to race against her best friend.

Both of them saw the beginnings of a great new game.

It could be every bit as fun as Chase was at the halfpipe.

Hannah waited for Brian at the top of the run.

There was no official way to start them, so they just counted to three.

"One, two, three!" they yelled, and off they went.

The early part of the course was full of sharp, high-banked turns that they both handled easily.

Hannah took a better path, and moved a little bit ahead of Brian.

Coming around the third turn, they ran into a series of moguls.

Brian kept his balance, bent his knees, and bounced over the small mounds quickly.

Hannah wasn't prepared for them and stumbled over the first few. She didn't fall, but losing her balance allowed Brian to pull ahead.

Over the next few straightaways and turns, Brian kept his small advantage.

He cruised over some angled bumps, or spines, making small jumps off each one.

Finally, he and Hannah navigated the last turn and headed down the steep, straight slope toward the finish line.

Only one jump remained. Brian took it hard, getting as much air as he could.

He loved to feel the rush of sailing high into the sky. Hannah did, too, but she knew that getting too much air would only slow her down.

She stayed low, sailing off the jump only a few feet but further down the mountain.

When they both landed, they were in nearly the same place.

When they crossed the finish line, it was too close to call.

They both skidded to a stop. "That was awesome!" Hannah yelled.

"Glad you liked it," came a voice. It was Zach. He was looking directly at Hannah. "Because it's going to be your last run."

THE NUMBER ONE RULE

Hannah and Brian couldn't believe what they were hearing.

Just minutes before, they had been so excited as they zoomed down the mountain.

Now, they were confused and upset.

"What?" Brian said, struggling to figure out what to say. "What do you mean? Why is it our last run?"

"Oh, not for you," Zach said. Then he pointed at Hannah. "For her."

Zach started to glide away on his board.

"Hold on a minute," Brian called after him. "What are you talking about?"

Zach stopped in his tracks. He spun back toward them. His face was angry, but he had a bit of a smirk, too.

"Look," he said. "I'll make this simple for you. Our snowboard cross team has one simple rule: No girls."

Hannah and Brian looked at each other, completely confused.

Hannah had heard from her parents about times when girls weren't allowed to do a lot of the things that boys were allowed to do.

But those times were long gone.

Hannah had never been told she couldn't do something just because she was a girl.

She had no idea what to say.

Brian was just plain angry.

"You can't do that, Zach, even if your mom is the manager!" he yelled. "That's discrimination!"

Zach laughed out loud. "I can do whatever I want," he said. "If it wasn't for me, there would be no team. And I'm not going to be caught snowboarding on the same team with any girls."

Brian was astonished. "Are you kidding?" he said. "You're kidding, right? Even you can't be this mean."

"It's not about being mean," Zach said.

"I want to win. Period. That's all I care about," Zach added. "And I can't win if I have a girl on my team."

Brian was trying to stay calm. He thought he might have a way to reason with Zach.

"Hey, man, you're making a mistake," he said. "Hannah's as good a skier and snowboarder as any of us out here. It shouldn't matter if she's a girl, as long as she's good enough. And she's more than good enough."

Zach's response was quick. "I don't care," he said.

Now Brian was back to being angry. "Well, I do care," he said. "I care a lot. And so do the other guys here."

Brian was moving toward Zach as he spoke. By the time he was done, he was in Zach's face. "If Hannah can't be on the team, then none of us will be, either," Brian said. "You won't have a team at all!"

Brian backed up a bit. He felt like he had made his point.

Zach let out a sigh. "Well, that would be a shame," he said. "Because my mom made a new rule at the resort: The only kids who get free snowboarding are the kids on the snowboard cross team."

CHAPTER 7

STANDING STRONG

Brian and Hannah were speechless.

Zach gave another sly smile, turned, and headed for the chairlift. "Time for another run," he said. "I need to get used to this new course."

As Zach sailed away, Brian and Hannah stood there, staring at each other.

Once again, they found themselves feeling like they didn't want to snowboard.

They glided back toward the chalet, unstrapped their snowboards, and walked inside.

Neither of them said a word. They walked to the snack counter and ordered hot chocolate. Then they found a warm seat in the chalet.

Hannah was a bundle of emotions.

She was angry at Zach for his new rules.

She was worried that her friendship with Brian was going to cost him his chance to snowboard.

And she was worried that she, too, was done snowboarding forever.

Finally, she found the words she wanted to say. "Brian, you've got to be on the team," she said.

"Not if you can't be on it," Brian responded.

"But if you don't, you won't be able to snowboard at all," Hannah said.

"I know," Brian said. "But what Zach's doing isn't right. We have to figure out a way to fight this."

"How can we?" Hannah said. "We can't ask our parents to help, because his mom is the new manager."

Both of them sighed.

Just then, the other kids arrived in the chalet. They had just run into Zach on the snowboard cross course, too.

"We heard about the snowboard cross team," B.J. said. "Sorry to hear you can't be on the team. We'll really miss snowboarding with you."

"What do you mean?" Brian said, rising to his feet. "Are you saying you are going to be on the team?"

"We have to," Will said. "Otherwise, we can't snowboard at all."

Hannah shrank into her seat. She couldn't even look at the boys.

"So you would turn on your friend, just to keep snowboarding?" Brian said. The anger rose in his voice.

"It's not our fault," B.J. said. "We didn't make the stupid rule."

Suddenly, Zach appeared in the chalet. "Are you guys coming?" he called. "Our first team practice starts in fifteen minutes."

The three boys looked back at Hannah and Brian. "Come on, Brian," Will said.

"I'm not going anywhere," said Brian.

The three boys left with Zach. None of them looked back to see Hannah's face.

Brian, his anger still bubbling on the surface, looked at Hannah. "I can't believe those guys," he said.

"Aw, forget about them," Hannah said. "You can't blame them for wanting to keep snowboarding."

"I know, but I'm not going to sit here and just take this," he said. "We have to figure a way to challenge this."

Suddenly, Hannah's face brightened. "That's it!" she shouted. "I'll challenge him! There's no way he'd back down from a challenge."

SHOWDOWN

Hannah and Brian bolted from the chalet as fast as they could.

They grabbed their boards and headed back outside and toward the snowboard cross course.

"Are you sure you want to do this?" Brian asked. "He's pretty good, and he's got way more snowboard cross experience than you do."

"I don't care," Hannah said.

They rushed to the chairlift and hopped on a chair.

The ride seemed to take forever.

As they rode up the lift, Hannah practiced the words she would say to Zach when she saw him.

When they hopped off the chairlift and headed to the course, they saw Zach right away.

He was at the top of the course, talking to the three other boys.

He was giving them advice on tackling the course.

Hannah cruised over to him and used only two words: "Prove it."

"Prove what?" Zach said. "I've got nothing to prove."

"Prove that I don't belong on the team," Hannah shot back. "Race me."

"Why would I do that?" Zach said.

"All I'm asking for is a chance," she said. "You win, and I won't bother you again. I win, and I'm on the team."

With that, the other boys chimed in.

"Come on, Zach," Ray said. "Give her a chance. It's only fair."

Zach took a deep breath. "Fine," he said. "Whatever. If I have to blow you away to make you stop complaining, I'll do it."

Hannah was a little surprised.

She hadn't been sure she'd be able to convince Zach to race her.

After all, he had nothing to gain by doing it.

As they moved over to the start of the course, Zach turned to his three new teammates. "I'll get this over with once and for all," he muttered.

At the starting line, Zach stared directly at Hannah.

Hannah looked a little nervous. But Brian gave her some final words of encouragement.

"Come on, Hannah," he said. "You can do this."

Will agreed to be the starter, and he counted to three.

The snowboarders took off quickly, but Zach got the faster jump.

He immediately cut in front of Hannah, nearly knocking her board off track in the process.

Zach held the early lead through the first set of hairpin turns.

Every time Hannah tried to move past him, Zach quickly changed his course to cut her off.

They zoomed around the third turn and into the moguls.

Brian could tell that Hannah had learned a lesson from her earlier run.

This time, she stayed low and let her knees absorb the bumps.

She zoomed to the outside of the track to try to pass Zach.

Zach again moved to cut her off, but this time he was too late.

Hannah was alongside him.

Still, Zach pushed outward.

Hannah neared the edge of the course and lost her balance.

Zach continued to push out until Hannah had no choice but to leave the course.

She tumbled off to the side as Zach continued down the hill, laughing.

Zach yelled, "Whoo!" as he cruised away.

Hannah didn't give up, even though she knew it was hopeless. She got back on her feet and back on the course.

By then Zach was two full turns ahead of her. Now, he was doing tricks on the run, showing off.

Hannah lost sight of him as she made the final turn.

He probably already finished the course, she thought.

But when she approached the final jump, she saw him.

He was sprawled across the jump.

He was reaching down toward one of his legs.

He seemed to be in a lot of pain.

Hannah slid up to him and turned her board to the side, coming to a stop alongside Zach.

"Are you all right?" she said.

"My ankle . . . my ankle," Zach said.

"Here, let me help you," Hannah said, bending down to grab Zach's hand.

Zach looked shocked. "Don't you want to win the race?" he asked.

"It's okay," Hannah said. "Let's get down the hill and over to the first aid office. Come on."

Zach was amazed.

Hannah just smiled.

She helped Zach to his feet.

Then she let him lean on her as they gently glided down the rest of the course.

Hannah turned to Zach after they crossed the finish line together.

"So, did I win?" she said, smiling.

Zach didn't say anything.

Hannah could tell he was thinking, hard.

Soon, Brian and the other boys joined them at the bottom of the hill.

None of them had seen what happened.

"Who won?" Brian asked urgently.

Hannah opened her mouth to speak, but Zach interrupted.

"She did," he said.

Only Zach and Hannah knew what really happened. Zach looked at Hannah, and then said, "She's on the team."

ABOUT THE AUTHOR

Bob Temple lives in Rosemount, Minnesota, with his wife and three children. He has written more than thirty books for children. Over the years, he has coached more than twenty kids' soccer, basketball, and baseball teams. He also loves visiting classrooms to talk about his writing.

ABOUT THE ILLUSTRATOR

When Sean Tiffany was growing up, he lived on a small island off the coast of Maine. Every day, from sixth grade until he graduated from high school, he had to take a boat to get to school. When Sean isn't working on his art, he works on a multimedia project called "OilCan Drive," which combines music and art. He has a pet cactus named Jim.

GLOSSARY

chairlift (CHAIR-lift)—a line of chairs hanging above the ground that carries skiers and snowboarders to the tops of the hills

chalet (shal-AY)—a lodge at a skiing resort, for visitors to go when they are not skiing

course (KORSS)—a track or route on which a race of some kind is run

frontside (FRUHNT-side)—a snowboard trick that starts with the rider facing forward

grind (GRYND)—to glide across a rail on a snowboard

halfpipe (HAF-pipe)—a U-shaped ramp used by snowboarders to provide a takeoff for jumps and tricks

mogul (MOH-guhl)—a mound of hard snow

rail (RAYL)—a bar that is raised above the ground that snowboarders use to glide across

straightaway (STRAYT-uh-way)—a straight course or track

MORE ABOUT...

Snowboard Cross is a relatively new sport. Snowboarding was a popular sport that grew into an Olympic-level competitive sport in the 1990s. But Snowboard Cross became an Olympic sport for the first time in the 2006 Olympics in Torino, Italy.

Unlike other snowboarding competitions, snowboard cross isn't judged.

Competitors race down a course, trying to beat each other to the finish line. Unlike other skiing events, competitors race against each other at the same time. Some people say it's a little like BMX bike racing, only on snow.

In the first rounds of the Olympics, snowboard cross racers make timed runs down the course. The racers with the fastest times make the final rounds, thirty-two racers in all.

... SNOWBOARD CROSS

The excitement grows in the final rounds, when riders race in groups of four. The top two racers in each heat make it to the next round, until only four riders remain. The final four ride in one last race, with the winner taking the gold medal.

Snowboard Cross was an instant hit in its first Olympics. Fans liked watching the riders compete on the course at the same time. The bumping and positioning during the head-to-head racing made it very exciting.

In the 2006 Olympics, American Seth Wescott won the gold medal for men. Radoslav Zidek of Slovakia won the silver medal, and Paul-Henri Delerue of France took bronze. In the women's final, Tanja Frieden of Switzerland won the gold medal, Lindsey Jacobellis of the U.S. won the silver medal, and Dominique Maltais of Canada earned the bronze.

DISCUSSION QUESTIONS

1. How do you think Zach could have handled the situation at the new resort better?

2. Hannah challenged Zach to a race to get on the team. How else could she have convinced him?

3. Will, B.J., and Ray chose being on the team over their friendship with Hannah. What would you have done? Did they have any other choices?

4. Why do you think Zach didn't want any girls on the team?

WRITING PROMPTS

1. Because of their parents' jobs, Brian and Hannah spent their time in a different way than most kids their age. Has your parent or guardian's job ever affected you? Write about it.

2. Brian stood up for Hannah. Write about a time when you stood up for someone, or when someone stood up for you.

3. Zach fell at the end because he was showing off. Write about a time when you made a bad decision and paid a price for it.

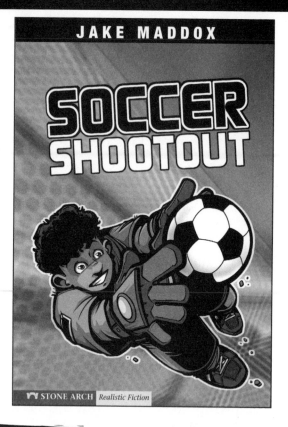

Berk always plays goalie for his soccer team. But when a new kid, Ryan, moves to town, Berk has to play an unfamiliar position. Ryan may have incredible talent, but he's also wildly unpredictable. Can the team survive the season?

BY JAKE MADDOX

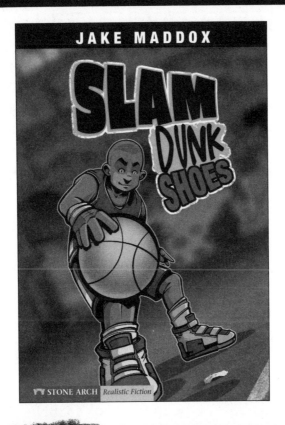

JAKE MADDOX

SLAM DUNK SHOES

STONE ARCH *Realistic Fiction*

Jamal's been asked to try out for a super-elite youth basketball team. His dad makes him a deal: If Jamal makes the team, he gets new shoes. But will the fancy new shoes really improve Jamal's game?

INTERNET SITES

Do you want to know more about subjects related to this book? Or are you interested in learning about other topics? Then check out FactHound, a fun, easy way to find Internet sites.

Our investigative staff has already sniffed out great sites for you!

Here's how to use FactHound:

1. Visit *www.facthound.com*

2. Select your grade level.

3. To learn more about subjects related to this book, type in the book's ISBN number: **1598898434**.

4. Click the **Fetch It** button.

FactHound will fetch the best Internet sites for you!